PEACE PEN PALS

HOPING FOR PEACE IN IRAQ

Divided by conflict, wishing for peace

by Jim Pipe

Gareth Stevens Publishing

Please visit our website, www.garethstevens.com. For a free color catalog of all our high-quality books, call toll free 1-800-542-2595 or fax 1-877-542-2596.

Library of Congress Cataloging-in-Publication Data

Pipe, Jim, 1966-
 Hoping for peace in Iraq / Jim Pipe.
     p. cm. — (Peace pen pals)
 Includes index.
 ISBN 978-1-4339-7732-9 (pbk.)
 ISBN 978-1-4339-7733-6 (6-pack)
 ISBN 978-1-4339-7731-2 (library binding)
 1. Iraq War, 2003—Peace—Juvenile literature. I. Title.
 DS79.763.P57 2013
 956.7044'31—dc23
                        2012006407

First Edition

Published in 2013 by
Gareth Stevens Publishing
111 East 14th Street, Suite 349
New York, NY 10003

© 2013 Gareth Stevens Publishing

Produced by Calcium, www.calciumcreative.co.uk
Designed by Paul Myerscough
Edited by Sarah Eason and Laura Waxman
Picture research by Susannah Jayes

Photo credits: Cover: Shutterstock: Gary Paul Lewis bl, Photosindiacom br, Mario Bono/Ryan Rodrick Beiler bg. Inside: Dreamstime: Imagecollect 42c, Jason Schulz 29t; Istockphoto: Craig DeBourbon 10b, 11tr, 15tr, 24br, 25tr, Sadık Güleç 16bl, 17t, Patricia Nelson 14b, GYI NSEA 8t, 9br, 18b, 26tr, 37tr, 38br, 43c; Peter Rimar 12tr; Shutterstock: Ilya Andriyanov 3, Homeros 36b, 41cl, Dan Howell 6bl, Sergey Lavrentev 10–11c, R. Gino Santa Maria 5bc, Olinchuk 5br, Samuel Perry 34b, Straight 8 Photography 33tr, Angel Simon 39c, Tomasz Wieja 10 background, Oleg Zabielin 32t; US Army: Master Sgt.Carl Mar 3cr, 31tr, Pvt. Emily V. Knitter 41cr, Charles Melton (USAG Fort Irwin) 45tr; US Department of Defense: 4br, 7c, 7br, 13br, Spc. Benjamin Boren 27cr, JO1 Lee Bosco 5t, Tech. Sgt. Michele A. Desrochers 22tl, Tech. Sgt. John M. Foster, U.S. Air Force 20br, Spc. Venessa Hernandez 19t, Petty Officer 2nd Class Andre N. McIntyre, U.S. Navy 21tr, LCpl Sarah B. Novotny 35tr, SPC Gary Silverman 28b, Master Sgt. Rob Trubia 44bc, SPC Jason Young 30b, Spc. Christopher Wellner 38tl; MC2 Edwin L. Wriston 22br, 23br.

All rights reserved. No part of this book may be reproduced in any form without permission from the publisher, except by reviewer.

Printed in the United States of America

CPSIA compliance information: Batch #CS12GS: For further information contact Gareth Stevens, New York, New York at 1-800-542-2595.

CONTENTS

Introduction: A Troubled Country	4
Chapter One: Invasion	6
Chapter Two: Civil War	16
Chapter Three: Daily Challenges	26
Chapter Four: Taking Control	36
Glossary	46
For More Information	47
Index	48

A TROUBLED COUNTRY

In recent times, Iraq has been in the news time and again. In 2003, a US-led invasion toppled Iraq's dictator, Saddam Hussein. Since then, the country has struggled to rebuild itself. Invasion also set off a bitter civil war. Hundreds of thousands of Iraqis have died, along with more than 4,000 US soldiers.

The country has seen almost constant conflict since 1979, when President Saddam Hussein came to power. In the last 30 years, Iraq has gone through three major wars, occupation by a foreign government, revolts, and terrorism. Though US forces have now left the country, the danger is not over. For many Iraqis, violence is still a part of daily life.

After the US-led invasion in 2003, foreign forces occupied Iraq until December 2011.

The Gulf War in 1991 was a disaster for Iraq. More than 100,000 Iraqi soldiers died and some 4,000 Iraqi tanks were destroyed.

Saddam's Rule

Saddam was a brutal ruler whose reign led to one crisis after another. Iraq has rich oil reserves, but Saddam spent the country's oil money in the 1980s fighting a long war against its neighbor, Iran. In 1990, he ordered his troops to invade another neighboring country, Kuwait. During the resulting Gulf War, through which Kuwait was liberated, Saddam's troops were quickly defeated by the United States and its allies.

Saddam stayed in power, but the United Nations banned Iraq from selling its oil abroad or buying goods from overseas. As a result, thousands of Iraqis died due to the lack of food and medicines in the 1990s.

IRAQ AND THE IRAQIS

Area of Iraq: 170,000 square miles (slightly larger than California)
Population: 30 million
Capital: Baghdad
Official languages: Arabic, Kurdish
Religions: Around 97 percent of Iraqis follow Islam

CHAPTER ONE
INVASION

In the 1990s, the United Nations believed Saddam Hussein was making deadly nuclear, biological, and chemical weapons, known as weapons of mass destruction (WMDs). When Saddam refused to let international weapons inspectors into Iraq, it led to his downfall.

The terrorist attack on the World Trade Center in 2001 completely destroyed the two buildings and killed thousands.

US President George W. Bush took action after the September 11, 2001, attack, when terrorists crashed two planes into the towers of the World Trade Center in New York City. The US government believed that Saddam Hussein had a connection to Osama bin Laden, the leader of the al-Qaeda terrorist group behind the 9/11 attack. This was never proved, but President Bush argued that Saddam was a serious threat to world peace.

Defeating Saddam

In 2002, a new UN inspection failed to find evidence of weapons of mass destruction. Even so, the United States and Britain invaded Iraq in 2003, bombing the country from the air. Then US and British forces invaded from the south, capturing the Iraqi capital, Baghdad. Within a month, Saddam had fled. Though there were still small pockets of fighting, the United States began to plan for Iraq's future.

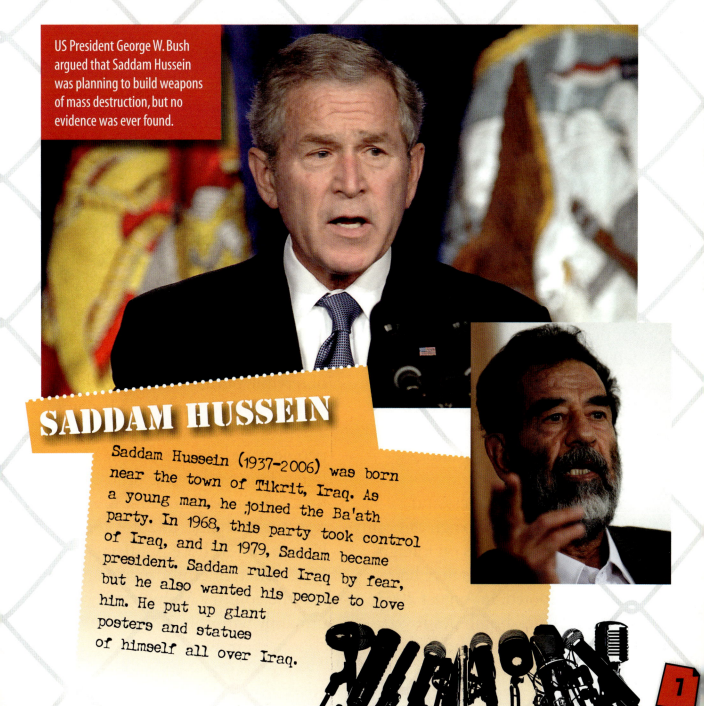

US President George W. Bush argued that Saddam Hussein was planning to build weapons of mass destruction, but no evidence was ever found.

SADDAM HUSSEIN

Saddam Hussein (1937-2006) was born near the town of Tikrit, Iraq. As a young man, he joined the Ba'ath party. In 1968, this party took control of Iraq, and in 1979, Saddam became president. Saddam ruled Iraq by fear, but he also wanted his people to love him. He put up giant posters and statues of himself all over Iraq.

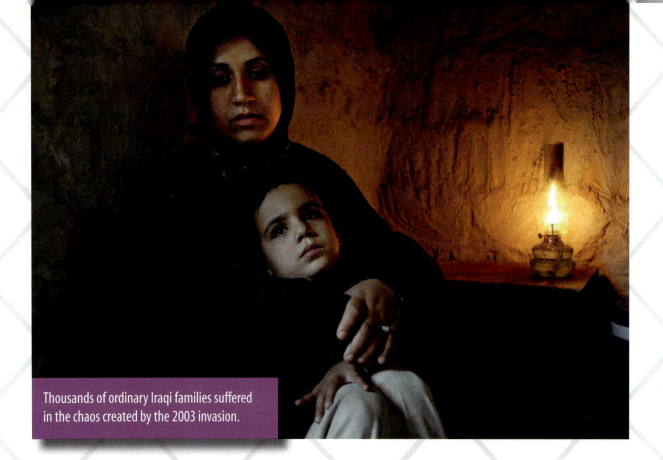

Thousands of ordinary Iraqi families suffered in the chaos created by the 2003 invasion.

Chaos on the Streets

The foreign invaders thought that most Iraqis would be happy to get rid of Saddam Hussein, but hopes for peace turned to despair as Iraq fell into chaos. With Saddam's army defeated, there were not enough troops or police to keep order on the streets. Mobs burned and looted government buildings.

Saddam's old supporters and soldiers began a campaign of bomb attacks and ambushes on foreign troops, using weapons they had hidden or looted. In August 2003, a massive truck bomb destroyed the United Nations headquarters. Many foreign aid agencies in the country decided it was too dangerous to stay and left.

Democracy in Iraq

During Saddam's reign, no one dared to vote against him for fear of terrible punishment. The United States wanted to help Iraq become a democracy, a country where people could choose their leaders freely. This would take time, so, at first, US diplomat L. Paul Bremer was put in charge. In 2004, the United States chose politicians from Iraq's different ethnic groups to run the country. Many Iraqis were unhappy with this. They wanted to choose their own leaders instead of those appointed by foreigners.

THE HUNT FOR SADDAM

US forces hunted down many of the leaders of Saddam's regime. They captured Saddam Hussein late in 2003. After a trial lasting several months, an Iraqi court found Saddam guilty of crimes against humanity in November 2006 and sentenced the former dictator to death.

US diplomat L. Paul Bremer tried to bring peace and stability to Iraq after the invasion, but the attacks on US soldiers continued.

FREE AT LAST

Baghdad, Iraq
April 2003
Dear Ethan,
 I'm so glad to be writing to you again. So much has happened in the last couple of months, as you have probably seen on the television. The first night the bombs began to fall in Baghdad, it was terrifying. Although my family lives in a suburb a long way from the city center, the huge explosions lit up the night sky and made the ground shake.

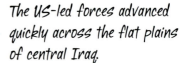

The US-led forces advanced quickly across the flat plains of central Iraq.

Communicating with the Outside

Under Saddam Hussein, many Iraqis were cut off from the outside world. Few had access to a computer, much less used it to go online or send emails. After the invasion, people were free to say or write what they wanted for the first time. Internet cafés sprung up all over Baghdad and other cities, and Iraq had its first bloggers.

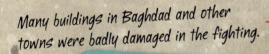
Many buildings in Baghdad and other towns were badly damaged in the fighting.

The next day, we moved to my uncle's house 12 miles from the city. Over the next few weeks, we hardly went out. On the radio, they said that Saddam's army was winning. My father didn't believe them—and he was right. A few weeks later we heard that US troops were in Baghdad. The war was over, and Saddam had run away. We returned home, and, luckily, our house was not damaged in the fighting.

Many people here are so happy that Saddam has gone. My family has been dreaming of this day, when Iraq is finally free. Though my country has suffered so much, with help from the outside world, we can solve our problems.

Sabeen

Insurgent Attacks

As the months passed, local fighters, known as insurgents, launched attacks on foreign soldiers. The insurgents wanted to drive US forces out of Iraq. They were soon joined by other terrorist groups linked to al-Qaeda.

Over the next few months, these terrorists killed hundreds of Iraqi civilians and police in a series of massive bombings, many in Baghdad. They also carried out kidnappings to attract media attention and terrify foreign workers in Iraq.

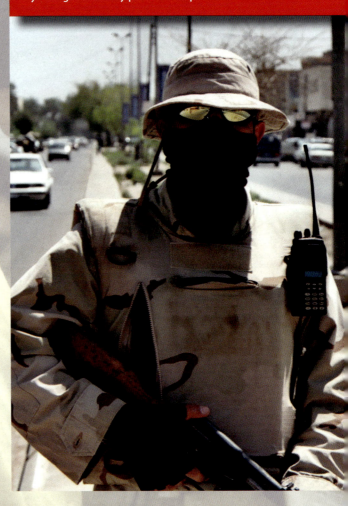

US soldiers were in constant danger of attack by insurgents as they patrolled Iraq's streets.

AL-QAEDA

The members of al-Qaeda in Iraq came from Arab countries all over the Middle East, such as Egypt, Syria, and Jordan. They followed a strict form of Islam and believed they were fighting a "holy war" against foreign, non-Muslim troops in Iraq.

Losing Iraqi Support

US forces launched several tough military campaigns against the insurgents. In a fierce battle to capture the insurgents' base in Fallujah, they destroyed large parts of the city. Though few civilians were hurt, many were angry that foreign soldiers were still at war in their country. When reports came out that some Iraqi prisoners had been very badly treated in the US-run prison of Abu Ghraib, this turned even more Iraqis against the occupying forces.

In 2005, Iraqis voted to choose new leaders to tackle their country's problems. The US government announced that US troops would begin to leave. However, this plan changed when a new wave of bomb attacks by insurgents began just a few months later.

Many Iraqis were very angry at the reports that US troops had abused Iraqi prisoners of war.

A TOUR OF DUTY

Jacksonville, North Carolina
September 2003
Dear Sabeen,
 It was great to get your letter. Like many people in the United States, I have been following the war on television. The news reports usually show our troops in action. Your letter reminds me of how scary it is for ordinary Iraqis caught up in the war.

It is a relief for families when soldiers return safely home.

The Forces in Iraq

The number of US troops in Iraq, known as "boots on the ground," has varied from 100,000 to 150,000. The invasion force also included 46,000 troops from the United Kingdom, as well as soldiers from other countries, such as Australia and South Korea. Turkey also sent 10,000 peacekeeping troops in 2003.

"Boots on the ground" in Iraq.

You know I said my dad was serving in the US Army? Well, a month ago his unit was ordered to go to Iraq. Dad said he was glad to be helping to make Iraq strong again. Although it was hard for all of us to say goodbye, Dad seemed confident that he'd be coming home again soon.

What I don't understand is why he needs to go at all. I thought the war was over. It sounds like most Iraqis were glad to be rid of Saddam Hussein and just want to live a peaceful life like folks in the United States. So why is the fighting still going on?

Write to me soon and tell me how things are changing in Iraq. I hope life has gotten easier for your family now that Saddam has gone.

Your friend,

Ethan

CHAPTER TWO
CIVIL WAR

The two Arab communities in Iraq, the Sunnis and the Shia, are both Muslim. They have been religious rivals for more than 1,000 years. In the recent past, the Sunnis had the most power and the best jobs in Iraq. Saddam Hussein was a Sunni, and the Shia suffered for many years under his rule. When the Shia rebelled after the Gulf War in 1991, thousands were killed by Saddam's soldiers.

After the overthrow of Saddam Hussein in 2003, the Kurds set up their own government in northern Iraq.

The Kurds

A third group, the Kurds, are not Arabs. Most Kurds are Sunni Muslims who live in the mountainous region of northern Iraq known as Kurdistan. They have their own language, culture, and history. At the end of the Gulf War, the Kurds also rebelled against Saddam but they were soon crushed. Millions of Kurds were forced to flee to other nearby countries.

Kurdish soldiers have worked alongside US troops to bring peace to Iraq, both in the north and in Baghdad.

After invading Iraq, the United States hoped the three groups could work together. However, in the elections of 2005, each group voted for its own political party. Although the Shia dominated the election, it took months to decide who would lead the new government. The Sunnis and Shia remained violent rivals throughout this period.

THE KURDISH REGION

At the end of the Gulf War in 1991, Iraq's Kurdish region was declared a safe haven. Since then, the Kurds have ruled themselves. Compared to the rest of Iraq, the region has prospered. Many new buildings have sprung up in the Kurdish capital of Irbil.

Sunni vs. Shia

There were already tensions between Shia and Sunnis. However, everything changed when al-Qaeda bombed the al-Askari Mosque in the Iraqi city of Samarra. Within a few hours, Shia militants were attacking Sunni mosques in Baghdad. In the following week, hundreds of Shia mosques were destroyed in revenge attacks.

More than 1,000 people died in the fighting that took place.

The situation in Iraq had suddenly become more complicated. Violence broke out everywhere and it was now Shia against Sunni, neighbor against neighbor. Meanwhile, attacks by al-Qaeda in northern Iraq killed 800 people and also destroyed more than 100 buildings.

The Tomb of Ali in Najaf, one of Iraq's holiest Shia shrines, was one of many mosques targeted by rival Shia and Sunni insurgents.

In 2007, US soldiers began using hi-tech testing devices to help them identify insurgents on the spot.

Troop Surge

To end the violence, in 2007, the United States sent an extra 20,000 troops to Iraq. By the following year, this so-called "surge," helped by Sunni fighters who had turned against al-Qaeda, had reduced the number of attacks. More and more areas were also being placed under the control of Iraq's own security forces. Yet Sunni militants continued to target the Shia community, leading to fears that the conflict could lead to civil war.

MUSLIMS IN IRAQ

Religion is an important part of Iraqi cultural life. Kurds, Sunnis, and Shia are all Muslims who follow the teachings of the Prophet Muhammad. Among their traditions are daily prayer, fasting during the holy month of Ramadan, and giving donations to the poor. A small number of Iraqis are Christians or Jews.

TERROR TACTICS

Baghdad, Iraq
April 2004
Dear Ethan,
 Last time I wrote, I was so full of hope for Iraq's future. Now life seems even more difficult than under Saddam. Even simple things can turn into big problems. My mom got a pain in her back, but we couldn't find a doctor. Then it got dark, and we had to wait until the next morning. By the time we reached the hospital, the pain was a lot worse. My mom is OK now, but we all had a scare.

Foreign soldiers need to win the support of the local people to beat the insurgents.

Under Attack

Bomb attacks can happen anywhere and everywhere: at a checkpoint, in a crowded marketplace, on a bus, or among groups of Muslims visiting a mosque or other holy place. No one is safe. In 2005, bombers even killed a group of children who were taking sweets from US soldiers.

Children who are friendly with US troops could be at risk.

The streets are very dangerous here. We only go out when we really have to. Every day we hear stories of bombs going off. Sometimes dozens of people are killed. Last week, US soldiers gathered near the entrance of our neighborhood with tanks and guns. We knew they were looking for terrorist bombers, but it is easy to get hurt in their fighting. We spent the night in our neighbor's "safe room," where they hid last year during the war.

Some people want all foreign soldiers to leave Iraq now. Without them here, I think the fighting would get even worse. We all hope that our country's new government will finally stop the war on the streets.

Small tracked robots armed with a video camera were used by bomb squads to help identify deadly IEDs (Improvised Explosive Devices).

Danger on the Streets

American troops in Iraq faced many hardships, from the threat of attack to the loneliness of being away from home. At first, most were stationed in large camps. The biggest of these were like small towns, with large dining halls, gyms, and a bus service.

After 2007, more and more soldiers were placed in smaller outposts in cities and the countryside. Some of the outposts were no bigger than a few tents surrounded by thick walls of sandbags.

Children playing on Iraq's streets have to watch out for broken glass, sharp pieces of metal, and bug-filled garbage as well as bombs.

On Patrol

Daily tasks for US soldiers included carrying out joint patrols with members of the Iraqi Army and police. They also met with village leaders. Tips from these citizens were a big help when searching for insurgents and hidden deadly roadside bombs.

Along with the danger of being attacked by insurgents or killed by bombs, troops had to deal with the hot, dry Iraqi climate. Temperatures can reach 110°F in summer, so air conditioning was essential. At the end of a long day, the soliders relaxed by playing cards, listening to music, or watching DVDs.

Military bases often have sports fields to help soldiers relax—and keep fit—in their spare time.

IEDS

One of the insurgents' main weapons is the IED, or improvised explosive device. Made from old cell phones and other electronic devices, these bombs are simple, cheap, and deadly. Most IEDs are buried near the roadside or hidden in objects such as drink cans.

WORRIED FEELINGS

Jacksonville, North Carolina
September 2006
Dear Sabeen,
    I was sorry to hear about your mother's back. I hope she is feeling better. How about you? I think about you every day when I see the reports of bombings in Baghdad. I don't know how you ever get to sleep at night when you hear guns being fired. You must be very brave.

US forces use special IED-clearing trucks to scan the ground to look for buried bombs and explosives.

Lifesaving Armor

Many US soldiers' lives have been saved by their body armor, which cushions a soldier from the force of a bullet, just like a catcher's mitt catching a baseball. In 2006, the military's Humvee vehicles used to carry troops on patrol were also given armor to protect them against roadside bombs.

All that heavy body armor can make you sweat in the hot sun.

Dad is home again at the moment and has told me about being out on patrol in your country. He tells me about all the body armor he wears, but it is hard not to worry. Most days, the television shows pictures of US soldiers who have been killed. We don't hear about it as much, but I know thousands of your people have also died in the bomb attacks.

I can understand why many Iraqis want foreign troops to leave their country. I'd feel the same if someone took over the United States. But why do the bombers want to hurt innocent people? Mom says they just want to show how weak the government is.

I hope that one day all the different groups in Iraq find a way to live in peace together. Then my Dad will come home for good, and you'll be able to play in the streets just like me.

Thinking of you,

Ethan

CHAPTER THREE
DAILY CHALLENGES

Violence and chaos in Iraq have forced more than 4 million people to leave their homes. More than a million Iraqis have fled to countries such as Syria and Jordan. Those who stay in Iraq face dangers and difficulties that make survival a daily struggle.

Many Iraqi families have been forced to leave their homes and stay with relatives or in refugee camps.

Living with Fear

Nearly everyone in Iraq has a relative or close friend who has died or been kidnapped by insurgents. People are afraid to step outside their front doors for fear of being shot or bombed. Workers and students risk their lives just to get to work or go to school. Kidnappers demand large ransoms (payments) from Iraqi families, and sometimes kill their victims even after they have been paid. Suicide bombers often target weddings, making it hard for people to enjoy the celebrations.

No Jobs

Unemployment is another big issue. One-third of the people in Iraq are without jobs. Meanwhile, one in four Iraqis lives in poverty. Despite monthly food rations, millions still go hungry. Even those with jobs are poorly paid and struggle to support their families.

Young children are suffering from a lack of safe drinking water and health care.

IRAQI REFUGEES

Life is also tough for many of those who tried to flee the fighting. Some Iraqi refugees were not allowed to enter neighboring countries such as Jordan and Syria. As a result, they have spent several years in camps on the border. Even those refugees who have found jobs and a new home miss their family, country, and their old life.

Basic Services

The US Army has helped to build new roads, bridges, sewage plants, and other basic services. However, violence has halted many projects. Years after the invasion, many Iraqis still have no access to clean water. They must either boil their water to make it safe to drink or buy bottled water.

Though Iraq is a major oil producer, there are often fuel shortages and long lines for gas. The electricity supply is also unreliable, partly because the pipes and cables are easy for insurgents to destroy. Even in the capital, many homes still have just four to six hours of electricity a day.

These Iraqi orphans are being handed presents and school supplies sent by aid agencies in the West.

In war-torn Iraq, parents were forced to choose between education and the safety of their children.

Health Care

Iraq's health system is slowly improving, but many hospitals, especially those in small towns and villages, are desperately short of equipment and medicine. It can take hours to see a doctor. More than half of Iraq's doctors and nurses have left the country since 2003. Militants also break into hospitals and kidnap doctors who treat patients from rival groups.

IRAQI WOMEN

In the past, women in Iraq had more freedom than those in other Arab countries, such as Saudi Arabia. They were allowed to have jobs and drive cars. Women could choose not to wear a veil or headscarf, which are traditional clothing for Muslim women. But since the invasion, thousands of women have been attacked by extreme Muslims for wearing un-Islamic clothing, having a job, or studying at a university.

SCHOOL IN BAGHDAD

Baghdad, Iraq
May 2007
Dear Ethan,
   Sorry it took so long to write back to you. There are many problems in Baghdad now, such as kidnappings and bombings, so I have to stay at home. I used to complain how awful our school was: the crumbling walls, the leaky roof, and the toilet that didn't work.

The students here are lucky—their school has recently been rebuilt.

Schools

More than 6,000 Iraqi schools have been repaired since 2003, and 60,000 teachers have been trained. However, roadblocks set up by US and Iraqi troops for safety make it very hard for students and teachers to get to classes. Many college professors have also stopped teaching after receiving death threats from insurgents.

Despite all the difficulties, many pupils love going to school.

At least being at school allowed me to forget everything else that was going on.

At first, I didn't mind being at home, but now I really miss my friends. I even miss some of the lessons (but not math!). In the morning, I do drawing or sing songs with my mother (I dream of being a pop star). I also help with the cleaning and cooking. In the afternoon, I am allowed to watch cartoons on television—if the electricity is working! Thanks to you, sometimes I get a chance to practice my English.

We hardly ever leave the house now. Things have gotten so bad, my mother and father are talking of going to live with my cousins in Syria. I can't imagine leaving my country and friends behind. Iraq is my home, for better or worse.

Sabeen

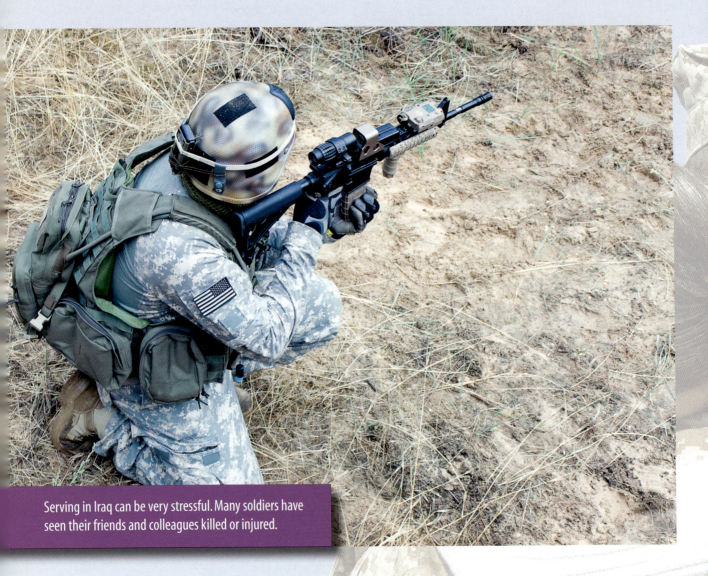

Serving in Iraq can be very stressful. Many soldiers have seen their friends and colleagues killed or injured.

Family Pressures

The war in Iraq brought great suffering to the Iraqi people. American families also suffer when their loved ones go off to fight—and when they return home. With around 150,000 US soldiers serving in Iraq, many families were directly affected by the war.

US soldiers fighting in Iraq were there for years at a time. Then they usually got a nine-month break before heading back. Some soldiers did three or four tours of duty in Iraq. This put a big strain on their families. Children missed their parents, and there was a lot of pressure on the parent left behind to bring up the family on his or her own. It was also very stressful for older parents who worried about their grown sons or daughters who were stationed in Iraq.

Missing Out

The parents fighting in Iraq often felt guilty for missing important family events, such as vacations, birthdays, recitals, and sports games. It was especially hard for mothers who had to leave young babies behind in the United States. They did not see their children for months at a time, and often they had changed enormously when they did finally see them once more.

It is heartbreaking for both parents and children when a mom or dad is away for several months on the front line.

WAR STRESS

The stress of being in combat and being in constant danger can have a long-term effect on soldiers. Many of them have seen friends killed or badly injured. When soldiers return home, it can also be very hard to get used to everyday life and become part of their family again.

MISSING DAD

Jacksonville, North Carolina
March 2008
Dear Sabeen,
   The news from Iraq doesn't seem to be getting any better. I hope none of your family or friends has been hurt in any of the bombings and other attacks that we hear about.

As the fighting in Iraq drags on, more and more people in the United States want to bring US troops home for good.

Phoning Home

The Internet makes it easier for soldiers serving overseas to keep in touch with family and friends. Even just a short email saying "hello" from a parent is enough to let the family know he or she is OK. Many soldiers would like a cell phone to call home, but it's too dangerous. Insurgents are able to listen in to calls or can track down where the caller is.

Email has made it a lot easier for troops to keep in touch with their families.

I know my life is so much easier than yours, but my dad has returned to Iraq, and every day he is out there feels like a challenge. I'm very proud of him, but I miss him very much. It was my birthday a month ago, and it just didn't feel the same without him. I can't wait until he comes home.

Dad is in one of the larger camps, and last week we learned that a rocket had been fired at it. We didn't hear from him for several days. It seemed like forever. When he finally got the chance to call us, Mom burst into tears. She was so happy he was OK.

Like more and more people in the United States, I just want the war to end. But I guess our soldiers can't really leave until their job is done and the worst of the fighting is over.

Your friend,

Ethan

CHAPTER FOUR
TAKING CONTROL

From 2007, many foreign troops began to withdraw from Iraq. Meanwhile, Iraqi forces started to take more control of the country's security, particularly in cities such as Basra. Since then, politics has slowly replaced violence. Will the new government be able to maintain peace?

Since 2003, hundreds of thousands of Iraqi soldiers and police officers have been trained by the US-led forces.

Bombs still explode and gunmen attack police checkpoints. Yet far fewer people are being killed than a few years ago. In the last five years, around 700,000 Iraqi soldiers and police officers have been trained. Most are Shia, however, and there are worries that many soldiers will not fight against the Shia militants still causing violence in the country.

A Struggle for Power
After years under Saddam's strict rule, the Iraqi people are now free to decide how their country is ruled. The new government is much fairer, but it is not fully in control of the country. Corruption is also a big problem throughout Iraq. While Sunni, Shia, and Kurds all take part in the government, each wants something different.

Car bombs remain a threat as Sunni and Shia groups battle for power.

Foreign governments are also involved in the struggle for power. The Sunnis are supported by Saudi Arabia and Syria. Iran, Iraq's old enemy, now has strong links with the Shia.

REFUGEE PROBLEM

Hundreds of thousands of Iraqi refugees remain scattered throughout Jordan, Syria, Lebanon, and Egypt. Many have no plans to return to Iraq because of the lack of jobs and the difficulty in getting back to their old homes. Others returned to Iraq then fled again because of the violence.

The price of food in Iraq has gone up in recent years, making life even harder for poor Iraqi families.

Industry and Farming

Iraq has few factories and few paying jobs outside the army or government. Nearly half of Iraq's land is suitable for farming, but many fields were damaged in the fighting. Because of this, basic foods, such as rice and wheat, must be imported from other countries. A series of droughts has also hurt farmers, forcing some to look for jobs in cities.

However, Iraq does have one of the largest oil reserves in the world. After the invasion, the oil industry struggled to get back on its feet, partly due to insurgents' attacks on pipelines. However, the amount of oil Iraq sells abroad has been growing steadily. In the future, this oil wealth could make a big difference to the lives of Iraqis.

Oil refineries such as this one could bring wealth and an improved standard of living to Iraq.

Free Speech

The Iraqi media has become a lot freer since the invasion. Newspapers and television stations report on issues such as government corruption, while comedies make fun of the government. Ordinary Iraqis write blogs or voice their feelings on radio phone-in shows. None of this would have happened under the rule of Saddam Hussein. Freedom of speech is now allowed.

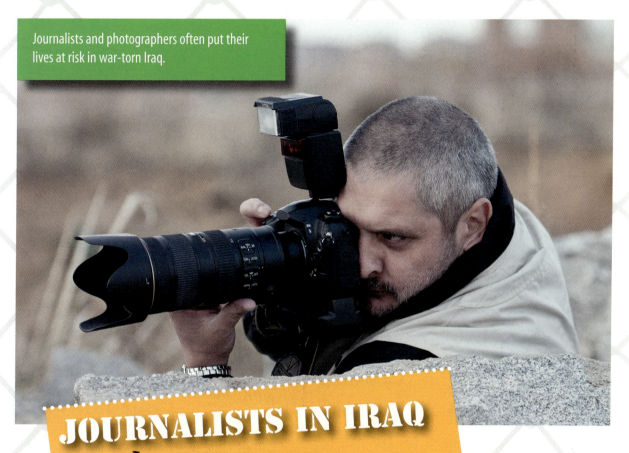

Journalists and photographers often put their lives at risk in war-torn Iraq.

JOURNALISTS IN IRAQ

Iraq is one of the most dangerous places in the world for journalists. Since the US-led invasion in 2003, more than 230 media workers have died, many of them Iraqis. Some were killed by crossfire while reporting. Terrorist groups such as al-Qaeda also targeted media workers, attacking their offices or planting bombs in their cars.

OUR FUTURE

Baghdad, Iraq
November 2010
Dear Ethan,

Here it always seems to be one step forward, two steps backward. Back in March, Iraq held elections to vote for a new government. My big sister, Amira, was very proud to vote for the first time. Militants tried to scare people away with violence, but millions of Iraqis still turned up to vote.

After the election, the Sunnis, Shia, and Kurds all accused each other of cheating. Then it took months for them to agree on a new government. Are they ever going to get along? I suppose we should be thankful there are elections at all. Ten years ago, a person voted for Saddam or risked getting a visit from his deadly secret police.

Right now, we Iraqis just want our lives back. We want to turn on the television and hear good news instead of how many people have been killed. We want to be able to open the door and walk through our neighborhood without fear. Some days, I worry this may never happen. But most of the time I am hopeful for the future. And I still dream that one day I'll be a famous singer! Maybe I'll write a song about my American friend who wanted peace just like me.

Sabeen

Better Goods

After the invasion in 2003, electronic goods poured into Iraq. Some 90 percent of homes now have a television, an electric cooker, and a refrigerator. Around one in four families owns a car.

Many Iraqis were very proud in 2005 when they voted in their nation's first free elections in more than 50 years.

When he became US President in 2008, Barack Obama promised to end the war in Iraq.

US Troops Leave Iraq

Early in 2009, US President Barack Obama announced the withdrawal of US soldiers from Iraq. As troops began withdrawing from Iraqi towns, a wave of car bombs struck government buildings in Baghdad, leaving hundreds dead. The following year, several hotels in Baghdad were also hit by car bombs. By the end of 2011, all US troops had left Iraq. Some believed that this change would help make Iraq more stable. However, others worried that the country could drift toward civil war.

In the capital, thick concrete blast-walls are still needed around important buildings. Military helicopters buzz overhead to patrol the city. Traffic jams are still caused by a maze of police checkpoints searching for bombs and insurgents. Most Iraqis believe these difficulties will be around for years to come. Stability in Iraq will be hard-won.

An Ordinary Life

There are few safe areas in Iraq but most people are doing their best to carry on their day-to-day lives. Once again, Iraqis in the capital can be seen sipping tea in cafés or shopping for books on the street. Parks on the banks of the Tigris River are crowded with families enjoying time together.

Though dozens of new newspapers appeared after the fall of Saddam Hussein, journalists who criticize the insurgents or the government are often threatened or killed.

COMMUNICATIONS

It is a lot easier for Iraqis to keep in touch these days. Before the war, only 80,000 Iraqis were cell phone users. Now there are almost 20 million, more than two-thirds of the country. There are also 1.6 million Internet subscriptions, compared with just 4,600 before the invasion.

HAPPY HOMECOMING

Jacksonville, North Carolina
December 2011
Dear Sabeen,

After waiting for this moment for years, finally Dad has left Iraq for good. It is so amazing having him home. His last few weeks in Iraq were the worst for us, with rumors that there would be lots more bombings as the final US troops left Iraq.

Some days, I look over at breakfast and can't believe he's sitting next to me. Dad doesn't talk about Iraq much, but he admitted he had a few

We are delighted that our troops are coming home.

Nine Years Later

When the final US troops left Iraq in December 2011, nine years after the invasion, the US flag was lowered in Baghdad. Many of the old US Army bases were left empty, like the giant Camp Victory, which was once home to 70,000 US troops.

It is great to be back together as a family!

narrow escapes from bomb attacks. We feel very lucky that he made it back OK. A few of his friends were killed, and several more were injured.

As our life gets back to normal, I think about you and your family. After all these years of writing to you, I feel sad that Iraq still has so many problems. If everyone there is just half as kind and brave as you, your country has a bright future!

One day I would love to visit Baghdad and meet you and your family. Or perhaps your dream of becoming a pop star will come true, and I'll get to watch your concert. For now, I will keep praying for peace in your country.

Take care,

Ethan

GLOSSARY

al-Qaeda a terrorist group once led by Osama bin Laden and responsible for the 9/11 attack on New York City in 2001

biological weapon a harmful biological agent that can be put into the air or water supply. Biological weapons can kill thousands of people very quickly.

blog a website containing a writer's own thoughts and comments, like a diary

checkpoint a place on a road or street where a security check is carried out. Also called a roadblock.

civil war a war between opposing groups living in the same country

crimes against humanity to kill or harm thousands of innocent people

election when people vote to choose a politician or leader

ethnic group people who share the same culture

hostage a person taken by force and kept until certain demands are met

IED (Improvised Explosive Device) a homemade bomb left on roadsides, used as a weapon by insurgents in Iraq

insurgent another word for rebel

invasion the takeover of a place or country, usually by military force

Islam a religion based on the teachings of the Prophet Muhammad and a belief in one god, Allah. The main religion in the Middle East, North Africa, and Central and South Asia.

kidnap to take someone away and hold them against their will

militant a rebel fighter

mosque Islamic place of worship and community center

occupy to take over a country

rebel someone who fights against something, often a government or other authority

suicide bomber a bomber who carries the bomb on their person or in a car and usually dies in the attack

terrorist a person or group who carries out violent acts against civilians to achieve a political goal

unemployment when people have no jobs

United Nations an international organization that includes representatives of most countries in the world, and which rules in cases of international dispute

weapons of mass destruction (WMDs) nuclear, biological, and chemical weapons with the power to kill large numbers of people

FOR MORE INFORMATION

Books

Friendman, Mel. *True Books: Iraq*. New York, NY: Scholastic, 2009.

Mason, Paul. *Timelines: Iraq War*. London: Franklin Watts, 2010.

Owings, Lisa. *Exploring Countries: Iran*. Minneapolis, MN: Bellwether Media, 2011.

Samuels, Charlie. *National Geographic Countries of the World: Iraq*. Monterey, CA: National Geographic Children's Books, 2007.

Websites

kids.nationalgeographic.com/kids/places/find/iraq
Find out more about Iraq.

www.kidskonnect.com/subject-index/26-countriesplaces/315-iraq.html
Discover facts and figures about Iraq.

www.classbrain.com/artfreekid/publish/article_37.shtml
Read lots of news reports and websites about the Iraq conflict.

http://www.infoplease.com/ipa/A0107644.html
Learn more about the history of the war in Iraq.

kids.yahoo.com/directory/Around-the-World/Countries/Iraq
Visit this website to find out much more about the Iraq war, the culture of the country, and what it is like to be a child in Iraq.

Publisher's note to educators and parents: Our editors have carefully reviewed these websites to ensure that they are suitable for students. Many websites change frequently, however, and we cannot guarantee that a site's future contents will continue to meet our high standards of quality and educational value. Be advised that students should be closely supervised whenever they access the Internet.

INDEX

al-Qaeda 6, 12, 18, 19, 39

Baghdad, Iraq 5, 7, 10, 11, 12, 17, 18, 20, 24, 30, 40, 42, 45
Basra, Iraq 36
Bremer, L. Paul 8
body armor 25
bombs 10, 21, 22, 23, 24, 25, 37, 39, 42
Bush, President George W. 6, 7

civil war 4, 16–25, 49

drought 38

education 27, 29, 30, 31
elections 17, 40, 41

Fallujah, Iraq 13
family life 10, 11, 27, 32, 33, 35, 45
farming 38

Gulf War 5, 16, 17

health care 27, 29
Hussein, Saddam 4, 5, 6, 7, 8, 9, 11, 15, 16, 20, 37, 39, 40, 43

Improvised Explosive Devices (IEDs) 22, 23
insurgents 12, 13, 18, 19, 20, 23, 27, 28, 31, 35, 38, 39, 41, 43, 45
Internet 11, 35, 43
invasion of Iraq 4, 6–15, 28, 29, 38, 39, 41, 43, 45

Iran-Iraq War 5, 37
Islam 5, 12, 18, 29

jobs 27, 29, 37, 38
Jordan 12, 26, 27, 37
journalists 39, 43

kidnapping 12, 27, 29, 30
Kurds 16, 17, 19, 37, 40
Kuwait 5

Lebanon 37

mosques 18, 21

Obama, President Barack 42
oil 5, 28, 38

patrols 12, 23, 25
prisoners of war 13

refugees and refugee camps 26, 27, 37

sanctions 5
Shia Muslims 16, 17, 18, 19, 37, 40
suicide bombs 23, 27
Sunni Muslims 16, 17, 18, 19, 37, 40
Syria 12, 26, 27, 31, 37

terrorists and terrorism 6, 12, 21, 39
Tikrit, Iraq 7

weapons of mass destruction (WMDs) 6, 7

3 2037 00079 7559

ELIZABETH TABER LIBRARY

DATE DUE

WITHDRAWN

DEMCO, INC. 38-2931